I0624727

Hot on the Heels

Astoria Wright

A Sassy Sleuth's Mystery

Book 1

Hot on the Heels

Copyright © 2019 by Astoria Wright

Published by Novelwright Press, LLC
Novelwright.com

Cover Art by James from Go On Write
GoOnWrite.com

Edited by 529Books
529Books.com

NOVELWRIGHT
PRESS, LLC

Table of Contents

Prologue

Sass in Diamond Springs

I live for the avant-garde, but I won't die for a trend—especially an ill-fitted corset. Modeling jobs range from excellent to egregious in the fashion world, but the agency makes all the difference. So, while fashion week in Milan and Paris were both world-class experiences, a photo shoot for an up-and-coming starter magazine in New York had me thinking my agent was out of her mind.

It was not the first time.

I doubted it would be the last.

I was tired of being the only model who spoke out about the conditions from which our contracts failed to protect us—the long hours, destructive diets, body shaming, lecherous men abusing their power.

Complaining wasn't an option, and no one would listen anyway.

What pushed me over the edge was the pure and unadulterated apathy I'd witnessed when a friend and fellow model became ill. The modeling agency ditched her in Milan and didn't care past her contract—voided by her eating disorder.

That's when I spoke up. Then the agency switched tactics, using fear and intimidation to try and get rid of me. They wanted me to think that my speaking up would keep me out of work, or that I was no longer viable as a model at the ripe old age of twenty-four.

I may be blonde, but I'm no dummy. I know that my strawberry highlights, green eyes, high cheekbones, and youthful skin won't last forever. I've been called many things before. From gangly teen to glam girl, no one's critiques stuck with me. The one thing a successful woman can never be is her looks alone.

However, I was beginning to feel like that was all anyone saw when they looked at me. So, even though I could try my luck signing with a better agency, I'd had enough. I wanted something else, something not driven by ageism and vanity.

In the back of my mind, I thought of the shimmering lake, the pristine pines, the picturesque Catskill

Mountains, and the many vacations spent with my grandparents. Whenever I felt unhappy, I thought of their home as my sanctuary.

Ever since the passing of my grandmother a summer ago, their home, which Grandfather affectionately called my grandmother's Petite Palace, that memory became more vivid each time I considered quitting. I couldn't sell the house, despite the many offers. The feeling lingered that it was meant to be mine.

I always trust my feelings.

With the corset cinched around my waist in a snake-like hold, I envisioned the Petite Palace as if I were standing by the oversized fireplace, feeling the warmth of the stone hearth. Though, that might be a full-blown hallucination from lack of oxygen. Once out of the corset—and out of my contract—I committed to my decision. I was going to Diamond Springs, New York.

Chapter 1
Corner on the Market

Blue Diamond Mall: soon to be the largest mall in the country. The halls sparkled. Glitter-trimmed poinsettias and icicle Christmas lights guided me past some of the most fashionable stores in the world to my destination. Despite its location—in the center of an otherwise small town—Sensational Soles carried everyday brands with prices that could compete with any chain store in America.

The moment my lavender pumps touched the ground, I could feel the positive energy. The sound of heels clicking against marble reverberated like the ding of a cash register and coalesced into a rhythmic pattern of success. I walked up to the main counter, pleased to see Sensational Soles' owner-manager, my longtime friend,

Ava Price. The moment she spotted me in my lavender trench-coat, she squealed and opened her arms. Ava sprinted around the marble counter corner and squeezed me so tightly; I thought I might bust a button on my Victorian floral top. I noted that despite the distaste for fashion she'd shown when we were teens, her flared jeans were in season. Then I looked down and noticed her wool ankle boots were a designer label. I beamed. It was further proof of her store's success.

"I heard you were coming back. I'm so happy you're here! When did your flight get in?" Ava said, letting me go and leaning against the counter.

It was so good to see an old friend exactly as I remembered her. I gripped my leather mini-tote as pure joy burst into my smile. "Eleven last night. But it was supposed to be a surprise. Don't tell me Scarlett told you?"

My godmother was usually good at keeping secrets. I wouldn't expect her to spoil the surprise, but all of my friends frequented her bookstore café and knew that I kept in touch with Scarlett no matter where I was in the world. She was part of the reason Diamond Springs was home to me.

"Ella bragged about you being 'fired,' which she heard from her many 'sources' in New York City. Scarlett couldn't help but set the record straight about you quitting. Of course, I pressed Scarlett to find out when you were coming home."

I couldn't keep my lips from rising further up my cheekbones. *Home.* I'd always thought of it that way, and even though I'd only ever seen her over summer and winter for eighteen years, I was glad Ava saw it that way, too. I hoped all my friends here did.

Frenemies were another story. Ella was one of those. Elanor Belle, "Ella Belle" to all her classmates and those unfortunate enough to participate in a pageant for a single day, was one of those. She'd held her nose higher around me since I dropped my first and only competition. I never bothered to explain that the crown meant much more to her than it had to me. But I also couldn't begrudge her attitude, since she'd lost her crown after I discovered her sabotaging the other girls in the competition.

"I'm sorry I ever introduced her to Diamond Springs," I said.

"Not as sorry as I am that she's the mall manager. Let's not talk about her or I'll lose my appetite. Are you free for lunch?"

"You read my mind," I said.

Hot on the Heels

Ava turned to her employee. "Sarah, do you have things covered here?"

The cashier in the long-sleeve, cranberry cardigan gave a thumbs-up and a *"yes, boss"* before Ava walked me to her office. It was only a few paces away at the back of Sensational Sole's first floor.

Orderly as expected, the room had a large oak desk, a filing cabinet, and a futon. It lacked a rug, curtains, and a coffee table. Shoe catalogs lay on the futon, and a pair of gorgeous pumps sat knocked over on the floor. I straightened them, admiring the work and the brand: Spark Heels. These were a luxury label and more expensive than I'd expected to see in a mall, but perhaps not outside the scope of Ava's wide-ranging collections.

I'd never seen this design before. It was a blush-pink pump with a rhinestone heel and a pink diamond embedded in the front. Beautiful as they were, I noticed a crack at the top of the right shoe where the glue had come apart.

"Forgive the mess. I swear we never transitioned properly from the old mall to this new space." Ava pulled her gray purse out of the bottom right desk drawer. I found it strange that neither the office nor the desk was locked, but then Ava had always been more trusting than me. She was more organized, too, and maybe a bit on the uptight side.

I chuckled. "Only you would call a few binders stacked neatly on a couch a mess. It looks like you had a long day yesterday."

Ava traced my eye to the shoes. "Oh, right, late nights. I'm preparing to launch a surprise."

"Oh?"

She grinned. "Nope, you're not getting it out of me yet. There are still a few kinks to work out, but I'll tell everyone as soon as I'm ready." She shut the drawer and walked with me, slinging the purse across her chest as we left the room.

"Have you seen the store?" she asked.

I shook my head.

She waved a hand. "C'mon, I'll show you."

We took a long route around the rows and the large shoe-tower displays. Around us, customers of all shapes, sizes, and colors trying on shoes on the storeroom floor made me proud of Ava's rise from business school to a businesswoman with prowess. Her inventory ranged from the everyday to high-end. Not a single section lacked shoppers today.

"You're doing a fantastic job. This place is amazing," I praised.

Hot on the Heels

Ava let out a dismissive breath as we turned out of the store and into the poinsettia-decorated walkways. "Talk about amazing: look at you! How many countries have you toured and ads have you done? And you look amazing in each one."

My smile faltered. "Yeah, well, that's all over now. But I'm so glad to be in Diamond Springs. I always pictured myself here one day."

Just not so soon.

We arrived at the concourse where escalators zig-zagged up and down four stories. A diamond chandelier scattered the sunlight on every level. I followed Ava up to the fourth floor. Tracing the gold rims of the escalator's guide rail, I couldn't help but admire the little touches.

"I don't remember anything like this kind of detail when I was growing up."

Ava's eyes wandered across the plaza and down a level. I couldn't read her expression but followed her gaze as far as I could to the downward-traveling escalators. All I saw were holiday shoppers. One of them stood out in an oversized rosy-brown sweater, green floral pants, a faux fur coat, and a wide brim, aquamarine hat. I couldn't see her shoes because of the bulky canvas shopping bags, but they were likely as mismatched. She held onto her hat as if she was aware of her fashion faux pas. It was no wonder she'd caught my eye, but I did question why the woman had captured Ava's attention.

"Looks like you've taken an interest in fashion," I said.

Ava looked forward just in time to step with me onto the fourth floor.

"Hmm? Sorry, my mind wandered for a second."

She couldn't help looking back at the woman. We made our way just to the left the fourth-floor escalator and Ava clutched the railing, watching. I noticed that the woman was holding her head, not her hat. Her hand moved to her chest, and she stumbled. Poor woman. She seemed ill.

Ava's face paled.

"Do you know her?" I asked.

Looking between the woman and me, Ava said, "No, I just happened to notice her."

"Should we go back see if we can help her out?"

"No," Ava said firmly. She ripped herself away from the railing. "You just got here. We should celebrate your arrival."

Despite the cheeriness in her voice, Ava's expression grew solemn. I waited for her to pick up the conversation. We walked past three shops and she still hadn't spoken.

"Are you all right?" I finally asked.

She took a short breath and looked at me. "Yeah, fine. You were saying something about the escalator?"

I blinked. That seemed like ages ago. It took me a minute to even think of what I'd been saying.

"I was just noticing all the detail that went into rebranding the Diamond Springs Mall, or the Blue Diamond, rather."

Ava's face relaxed. "You haven't been here since the transformation. All those years of construction are paying off." She grimaced. "For some of us more than others."

She looked past me to the shop we were approaching: Glamshoe Maven. I noted the diamond-studded border on the digital sign and the black marble floors, which were recently waxed, based on the yellow signs scattered around the part of the shop I could see. The shoe racks, rather than silver, were a tacky gold.

"Your competition?" I asked.

"The largest shoe store in Blue Diamond Mall. It has two floors instead of one. But so will we soon."

Ava headed to a restaurant on the very edge of the food court called the Savvy Palate. A waitress brought us to one of the many black tables with eggshell-white chairs. The absence of color contrasted nicely with the pops of pink. I thanked the waitress for the coral-colored menus. Ava flipped hers over numerous times.

I eyed her jittery fingers. I made small talk to pass the time until I could turn the conversation to deeper questions. Halfway into our meal, I found my opening.

"I'm so glad you're back. It's fantastic to see an old friend, especially you. You always had a way of making me feel like everything in the world was OK," Ava said.

"Scarlett suggested on the phone that you were the first person I should see."

"Oh? Why's that?" Ava was concentrating on her salad. I had a feeling she was avoiding eye contact.

"Maybe for the same reason you just said. To help you feel that everything will be OK."

The comment earned me a glance from Ava, but nothing more.

I set my fork down. "Ava, what's wrong?"

A smile flitted across her face. "Wrong? Nothing, just business stress. I've been overworking—that's all. It's good to have a break."

Her expression told me there was more to the story, but this was just the beginning of my stay in Diamond Springs. I'd have plenty of time to find out what was on her mind. *She'll tell me when she's ready.*

I picked up my fork. "You know, I'm not surprised about your success. I knew the minute you took over your parents' shop, you'd make it bigger than ever. You were, what, number one in your business school?"

"Two, unfortunately. But I won't take second place next year. Sensational Soles will outdo GlamShoe Maven within a year. I have it all planned out."

Chapter 2

Shop Till You Drop

We passed GlamShoe Maven on the way back to Sensational Soles. This time, Ava did not look at the sign but walked back at an eager pace. She apologized several times for the hurry as she went.

"I was so excited to see you; I lost track of time. I have an appointment with a…with someone that I can't miss."

"Of course, I understand," I said as I kept pace.

We came to an abrupt halt as the fourth-floor escalator took us down to the third level. Shoppers crowded around the promenade, pushing their way toward a look at something below. Ava pushed past the crowd with her polite battery of *"excuse me's"* and *"pardons."* To the right, I spied an opening beside a flowerpot. Tapping Ava's arm, I cocked my head in that direction. Ava nodded, and we nudged forward until we could touch the railing.

Police tape stretched around a fountain below. Onlookers watched the men in blue as they made way for a stretcher. Even from three stories up, I knew the woman lying half in and half outside the water was not going to a hospital, but a morgue.

Ava gasped. Light from the glass roof splintered off the chandelier as if shining directly on the woman's gold earrings, the faux fur coat, and the mix of pink and green we saw earlier. I looked to Ava, who seemed genuinely horrified. I put my arm around her, fighting the dread twisting in my stomach.

Ripping herself away from the railing and pushing herself through the bystanders, Ava made it to the empty escalator and headed down. I dashed to keep up. I wanted to ask why she was heading straight for a crime scene.

Ava stopped at the police tape, eyeing the pumps on the woman's feet.

The sick feeling rose to my throat. The woman was wearing a pair of simple, elegant pumps with a pink diamond heel. It was the same pair I'd seen in Ava's office.

"Ava, what's—"

She snatched my wrist. We walked briskly away from the crime scene and did not stop until we were safely in the confines of her office. She closed the door behind her, and her eyes flew to the spot where the heels had been.

They were gone.

Ava paced. I winced, wishing there was something I could do.

"Who was the woman?"

Closing her eyes, Ava let out a long sigh. "That woman was an employee of Sensational Soles. Her name is Penny Hollison."

I felt numb as Ava walked across the office and fell into her chair.

"You were worried all through lunch—ever since you saw her. Did you know something like this was going to happen?"

Ava dropped her head into her hands. "No. Of course not."

She sat like a statue, staring at the desk. I leaned forward, speaking softly, "Ava, I think you'd better tell me what's going on."

Ava dropped her hands. "I fired her a week ago. She was stealing merchandise for herself and information on my company for my competitor." She pointed upstairs.

"Information like what? Balance sheets?"

"That, my merchandise providers, and other things."

"Those shoes, they were—"

"Yes, that's what worries me. They were part of an exclusive deal I was negotiating with Spark Heels. Those shoes were one of a very small shipment of experimental heels. They weren't ready for market yet. And hers were damaged, which might look like sabotage."

"No one would blame you for that. It was obvious they were broken. She should've noticed that before stealing them." I looked at where the shoes had been on the floor. Even the magazines looked like they'd been disturbed. "Ava, I noticed you didn't lock the door when we left. Nothing in your office seems to be locked. Why is that?"

Ava gestured toward the office as a whole, "I have nothing to hide. I never lock this door. My merchant lists are not exactly a secret since they make deliveries directly to my shift managers and, yes. My books are sensitive information. But my head manager, Sarah, she's a whiz at math. She's helped me with the records before, so even that isn't locked away at all times. In theory, my employees could gain access to anything."

My eyebrows furrowed. "You've always had a cautious nature. I'm a little surprised you don't keep your records locked away."

"I sort of misplaced my keys since…well, for a while. The money is accounted for and deposited every day. But the documents? I guess I didn't expect anyone to steal *information.* Anyway, I caught Penny, and she confessed. She wanted to keep her job, and she offered to spy on Marge for me."

"Marge?"

"Margaret Maven, a.k.a the GlamShoe Maven."

I gasped. "You didn't…?"

"Never. I'm competitive, but I'm not underhanded. I fired her on the spot, and I confronted Marge about it the same day."

"What happened when you confronted her?" I asked.

"Nothing. She, um, she had passed away."

My eyes widened. Ava saw my surprise and answered my unspoken question.

"She had a heart attack before I ever got there. It was natural causes. Terrible timing. Anyway, the store belongs to her brother, Drew, now."

"So, Penny is caught stealing for Marge, then Marge dies and Penny shortly after?" I asked.

"It sounds suspicious when you put it like that. Marge was only forty-eight, but I didn't think there was anything unnatural about it at the time. Heart attacks happen to adults of all ages. But with Penny.... Do you think it was murder?"

"Not necessarily. She looked ill. And her heel was broken—she could've fallen. Or she may have jumped. We don't know anything until the police investigate."

As if in response to my statement, a knock sounded on the door. Without waiting for an answer, a woman burst through the room and locked eyes with Ava. Ava sat up straighter.

"How dare you? You have no right to barge into my office like this," Ava said.

"It's my office as long as I run this mall," said the woman with the auburn hair and sky-blue eyes. She turned to her side and allowed an officer to pass her. "There she is," the woman said.

I stood. It had taken me a minute to place her.

"Ella? Ella Belle?" I asked, recognizing her despite the new hair color and what looked to be an expensive nose job.

Ella paused, then regained her breath, and one of the smiles she reserved for making people feel like trash. The police officer had no time for our reunion. He addressed Ava while the second officer gestured for us to leave the room.

"Miss Price, we have a few questions for you," was all I heard before Officer #2 closed the door.

Outside, Ella crossed her arms, saying, "Kaitlynn Sasse. I knew I would see you sometime soon. I didn't imagine it would be standing next to a murderer. If you're *not* involved in this, you would be wise to stay away." She said *"not"* as if she was certain that the opposite was true.

"You would be wise not to accuse people of murder. That's libel."

"Not if it's true." Ella's hands moved to her hips. Her artificial fingernails dug into her sides. I had barely said two sentences, and already I was under her skin. *Good.*

"Drop the act, Ella. You and I both know Ava well enough to know it isn't true. If you want to play the intimidation game, do it with someone who's actually guilty, or leave the investigation to the real authorities. Neither Ava nor I are afraid of you."

Ella's nostrils flared. "I'm not a model like you, Kait. I don't play dress-up. I have *real* authority over all Blue Diamond employees…and all criminals, and they have good reason to fear me."

"Is that a threat?" I asked.

"A warning," she said, adding, "I will prosecute them to the extent of the law."

"The criminals or your employees?" I asked.

She balled her fists. Swiveling on a tacky tan heel, she stormed away. I frowned as she left. Part of me felt for her. In the back of my mind, I had always hoped one day she could once again be the person I befriended years ago. Before the beauty pageants, school pressures, business shrewdness, and all the trappings of wealth that she'd apparently fallen into, there had been a girl who'd share her food at lunch and exchange stories about home with me. That Ella Belle—originally from Georgia and would never let you forget it—was gone.

When the officers left, I could hear Ava sniffling.

The older officer stopped to ask me, "You're Miss Sasse?"

"Yes."

"And you can confirm that you were at lunch with Miss Price at, uh…" He looked in his notepad and pulled the name to his tongue. "The Savvy Palate?"

"Yes. Sir, if I may, the mall has security tapes of all main areas. You can see the cameras on every ceiling corner. If you got a tape of the concourse, you should be able to see Ava wasn't anywhere near the crime scene. She had nothing to do with the fall."

The gray-haired man, Officer Hart, closed his notebook. It was disconcerting how he studied my face. I almost felt like he would accuse me next.

"We checked the tapes," the younger officer—*Jones,* his badge read—responded.

Thankful for the interruption, I asked, "And?"

"It wasn't a clear shot. With the seasonal shoppers and the cameras rotating, it was hard to get a clear sight of the attack."

Officer Hart gave him a side-eye glance and added, "We're still reviewing the tape, before and during the fall, so if there's anything on it, we'll catch it. And, as observant as you are, you'll note we never said Ava was involved."

"Then why question Ava? Why not just stick to the tapes and the witnesses?"

The older officer slid the notebook and pen into his shirt pocket. "Due diligence. *If* she or anyone is involved in Miss Hollison's death, we'll catch them. It's only a matter of time."

The officers left it at that. As they exited the store, I reopened the door to Ava's office. She sat there, blinking, her eyes puffy and red. She looked up when she noticed me standing across from her desk.

"They think I did it, Kait. I know it."

I rested my hands on the desk and leaned in. "They have no reason to believe you did anything but fire Penny a week ago."

"But she was supposed to come in this morning to get her last paycheck. I told my employees to hand Penny the paycheck and then keep her out of this store—by any means necessary. I didn't mean *kill her*."

I smiled sympathetically. "No one interpreted it that way, I'm sure. And she wasn't in your store when she died."

"She was right before that, though. Do you know how that looks? And the shoes on her feet—God, some of the shoes I saw had fallen out her bags! She was stealing from me right before she died."

I folded my arms and put a hand to my chin. It didn't look good, but at least the officers had confirmed they didn't even know if the woman had been pushed. But a twenty-something doesn't just steal from an ex-employer and then leap to her death with the goods still in hand.

"Oh God, this is bad, isn't it?" Ava asked.

I had to admit it was, but not aloud. "It'll be all right. I know you're innocent. The police will see that, too."

Chapter 3

In the Red

Home has many definitions for many people. To me, it wasn't a penthouse, a school dorm, or apartments in Milan, Paris, London, or New York. It was a two-story, stone home built to my grandfather's specifications as a present to the woman he loved—my grandmother. My father, along with his many mistresses over the years, tolerated my mother's presence for the sake of appearances. But my grandfather had doted over my grandmother. He denied her nothing.

He could afford to do so with his architecture firm and his eye for detail. So, with careful consideration, he designed everything from the stonemason work of the walls to the wood medallion on the glossy hardwood floors. Even the white, maple kitchen with hand-carved cabinets spoke of my grandmother's love of the elegant.

Hot on the Heels

I placed my trench coat on the Victorian, mahogany coat rack and walked past the curving staircase to the sitting room. Lighting up the fireplace, I sat a moment on the mauve, Parisian tufted sofa. Just like the wood in the fireplace, my mail had been placed on the coffee table by the housekeeper who came a few hours daily to tidy up. I separated the letters from the fashion magazines, sorting through the envelopes for any good news.

One stood out from Titania Talent Agency. I hesitated. It might have been a job offer, but I wasn't sure I wanted to go back into modeling. I'd come out here for a fresh start and hadn't had time yet to find myself or to allow myself to feel lost.

The doorbell disturbed my thoughts. That bell chime made me grin as I went to answer the door. For so many years that sound had meant guests arriving for dinner parties, or nights out, or just friends chatting over tea and cake. My grandparents had always had a butler to answer the door, but he'd retired, and since I was new in town, there was only me to answer it.

I peeked out the window as I always did when I was alone. Standing there was perhaps my favorite person in all of Diamond Springs. My lips could not have stretched wider as I opened the door.

"Scarlett!" I reached for a hug.

She squeezed her arm around me and said, "Kaitlynn Sassy-As-Always, you're back!"

I blushed at the nickname Scarlett had given me as a child. She was my mother's age and had been a friend of hers once upon a time before the city had changed Tessa Denworth into Tessa Sasse. Scarlett kept her hometown values and her adoration of my grandparents. She'd become my second mother whenever I came out here.

I invited her in, and she went straight for the kitchen, insisting on putting on tea. She made her way around the cabinets naturally, having visited with my grandparents for years. I knew before she'd chosen that she would pull out the orange spice tea bags and the autumn floral cups.

"I have to thank you for taking such good care of Grandma Rose this last year. She said your visits were the highlight of her week," I said as we sat at the white, Maplewood table.

She lifted her cup, saying before she sipped, "I only wish it had been more often."

"You have a bookstore to run. How is Sycamore Books doing?"

"Dying, like most other bookstores this century. I should've closed it years ago, but as long as there's profit, I can't seem to part with it."

Hot on the Heels

"I'm sorry. I thought with the mall expansion, things would get better."

"That's true for some, especially anything taking the title *"largest in America."* Blue Diamond wants to become the largest mall in the USA, so shops like mine are being pushed out unless we can prove that we can compete with the chain stores Ella wants to attract."

I sipped the tea and considered the implications of what Scarlett was saying. I knew Ava's competitive spirit, but I also knew how Ella could bring out the worst in people. The mention of her made the hair on the back of my neck raise.

"I saw her today," I said.

Scarlett scoffed. "Worse, isn't she? That chip on her shoulder is turning her whole heart to wood. But she's not the one I came here to talk about."

"You didn't just come to see me?" I asked.

"That too, but no, I need to talk to you about Ava."

"I was with her this morning. I know about Penny and her connection to Sensational Soles."

"Unless you were with Officer Hart ten minutes ago, you don't know that she's officially at the top of the list as a person of interest."

My first thought was to wonder why Scarlett had been with Officer Hart, but I could guess the answer without asking. They were both about the same age living in a small town. I hadn't seen a ring on his finger, and Scarlett Sycamore was still as pretty as a ray of sunshine with her golden skin, hazel eyes, and curvy figure.

But her relationship with Officer Hart wasn't my main concern. What she'd said about Ava made my heart beat unnaturally fast. I pushed the tea aside.

"Any idea why he suspects her? I mean, why not suspect Marge Maven's brother? Her death is suspicious, too."

"Her passing was ruled to be natural causes. And Marge's brother, Drew, was devastated when Marge died. True he inherited Marge's shop, but he was overwhelmed by it. He had to hire an assistant to keep things straight. And he has a soft heart, according to Ava. He even hired a girl with shoplifting tendencies."

"Why would he do that?"

"I'm sure he wanted to give her a second chance. The Mavens were good like that. Poor Ava. She always competed with GlamShoe Maven even when I said they'd be more productive if they'd teamed up. I mean, Marge's shoe store was a huge success."

Her comment about shoplifting got me thinking. That woman looked like she was wearing too many layers, even for a winter day. And she was wearing a pair of stolen pumps.

"Did she ever steal while she was working for GlamShoe Maven?" I asked.

Scarlett frowned. "Apparently, she was at it again the day she died, stolen shoes, clothes, jewelry, you name it from all sorts of stores."

"She certainly had a lot of shopping bags. Maybe someone caught her stealing, and she panicked and fell?"

"Not as far as I know. It's possible, I guess."

"More plausible than Ava killing her. Was there any particular reason Hart suspects Ava?

"Jasper, er, I mean Officer Hart, can't tell me anything since it's an open case. I'm not even supposed to know Ava is a suspect. I think he let it slip because he hopes it isn't true, which at least gives you some advantage in gathering evidence about her innocence."

"Me?" I asked.

I had promised Ava I would support her, but I hadn't expected Scarlett to put me on the case, so to speak. I wanted to help, but I didn't know the first thing about police investigations. I told her so.

"Kait, I've known you all your life, and you have one of the sharpest minds I know. Plus, I have someone in mind to help."

"Who?" I asked.

She lifted her brown leather bag off the chair and removed a card. I flipped it in my hands and read the front. "Aeson 'Ace' East, Private Investigator?"

"The best on the East Coast. If you truly want to help Ava, he's your best chance."

Chapter 4

Detectives and Window Dressings

The trench cape might have been overdoing it. With my glossy red Mary Jane heels, beige, knee-length dress, and checkered red and beige cape, I looked like a mannequin in a store window. But I thought of that as a compliment.

Private Investigator Aeson East sized me up with one look. A smug smile appeared on his face—not the cringy kind that made me want to slap a man for incivility, but the annoying kind that judged a woman and dismissed her before she'd said a word. *He and his faded navy-blue pants and wrinkly light-blue shirt combo had better not be judging anyone.*

Of course, he was undeniably handsome. Even with the scruffy five o'clock shadow at noon, he had a masculine appeal. His dark hair contrasted with his ash-gray eyes so that they dared and invited one to meet his gaze.

Ignoring his look entirely, I walked right up to the counter where he stood with his arms crossed. He stayed as he was, leaning back against the counter beside the coffee pot.

"Ace East? I'm Kaitlynn Sasse." I reached out a hand.

He turned his back to me, pouring his morning coffee. My eyes widened. He didn't miss my expression, just as I hadn't missed his gray eyes looking at my reflection through the metal espresso machine.

"It's P.I. East, if you don't mind. What can I do for you, Miss Sasse?" he asked.

He could have offered me a cup of coffee, asked me to sit down, or any of a wide range of courtesies a normal man would have observed for a lady. His tone wasn't sharp, at least, but he gave off the distinct vibe of a no-nonsense, all-business attitude. It didn't matter. I'd dealt with Ella for years; I could handle him.

I sat uninvited in the chair opposite at a desk I assumed was meant for a secretary. It faced the front door, and the office behind it had *P.I. East* inscribed on the door window. East didn't seem bothered by my move, but I had to turn toward the counter to see him since he made no effort to move toward me.

Hot on the Heels

I barely covered my annoyance as I said, "I have a case for you." He sipped his coffee. The corner of my mouth slanted in dismay, but I continued, "A woman fell to her death in the Blue Diamond Mall yesterday."

"I heard about that."

"Then you know the police think it might have been a homicide."

"It was," he said.

"How do you know?"

He shrugged. "She landed face up. People heard her screaming as she fell. That means she was either pushed or fell accidentally. And since the entire railing was intact where she fell, pushed seems more likely."

Brilliant. I hadn't thought of the railing. Despite his manners, it was clear there was a reason he was one of the most sought-after private investigators on the East Coast. As far as I was concerned, he'd just proven he could do the job.

"So, how does this work? Is there a contract I sign to hire you?" I asked.

"Hire me? You're jumping the gun. I never said I would take the case."

I narrowed my gaze, expecting some sexist reason or other.

"Why not?" I asked.

"I'm overloaded as it is. If you were applying to the open secretary position, I'd still barely have time interview you. I'm sorry, but I can't take any cases right now."

With his manners, I wasn't surprised by the lack of help. He struck me as a man with little patience, or he was milking me for extra money for his precious time. I digressed.

"Money is not a problem for me, Mr. East," I offered.

"Good," he said, "because it's not a problem for me, either. As I explained, *time* is the issue. I'm afraid I don't have any to spare."

I stood and pointed to the desk. "You would if you gave those two cases to a bounty hunter, then took a fee for the referral and for any information you already uncovered that you could pass his or her way. And since money isn't an issue for you, the referral fee should balance out the time you've already spent on it."

Ace glanced down. He didn't bother asking how I knew there were two open investigations to find the whereabouts of a suspected arsonist and a missing husband who'd hired a hitman against his wife. The paperwork for both sat open in plain view on the desk.

Ace walked over and closed the manila files. He set his coffee cup beside the papers. Then he took a seat and leaned back in the chair as far as it would go. His hand covered his square jaw, and his eyes studied me with…amusement? He tilted his chin, then nodded.

"All right. I'll come with you to the crime scene. I'll give you what observations I can, and if a case develops, I'll shuffle some cases around to take yours."

I smiled. "You're on, P.I. East."

I half expected him to tell me he liked my spunk with the way he smiled.

"Call me Ace."

Chapter 5

Hitting the Shops

Mr. East, a.k.a. Ace, bent over the fountain with the crime scene photos in hand. He glanced between them. Whatever he thought he might see was beyond my patience.

"I'm telling you, the police went over every inch of this place. You have the list of items they found right in front of you. We should be questioning people involved in Penny's life, not re-examining what we've already seen," I said.

Ace reached into his pocket and took out a black pen. Rather than taking notes, he rolled up his sleeve. He used the pen to scoop something out of the bottom of the fountain. I walked closer. Ace held it up for me to see. Looped around the pen was a diamond ring.

"The police missed this," he said.

Hot on the Heels

I held the pen while he went to his bag. "I know this ring, or the brand anyway. This is a Zazbry ring."

Ace brought a mini, plastic bag over to hold the ring without contaminating it. Before handing it over, I held it up to the light. There was something engraved in the band.

"Love always, Marc," I read before sliding the ring into the bag.

Ace sealed it and placed it back in his suit jacket pocket. "Looks like there's a boyfriend."

"Or a fiancé," I countered.

"Either way, I think we need to check out any Zazbry's in the area. Maybe we can find out who bought this."

I walked to the directory. Ace placed the satchel across his torso and followed. It took just a moment to find that Zazbry's was only a stone's throw away from Sensational Soles.

"It's on level three by the main department store," I said.

"Let's go."

Ace headed toward the escalator and I hastened my step.

"So, no serious relationship yet. Am I right?" I teased as I stood beside him on the escalator.

He raised an eyebrow.

"Every man I know gets to know where the jewelry shops are when things get serious," I explained.

Ace looked away. His attention seemed to focus on the moving steps above us. I looked away too. I'd meant it jokingly, but he didn't seem to appreciate the humor.

"Sorry. Too personal. I understand," I said.

At the top of the escalator, he finally responded, "Zazbry wasn't here at the time." He put his hands in his pockets and quickened his pace.

"I'm sorry, how long ago was it?"

I waited for his response. Just when I thought he wasn't going to answer, he stopped.

"You were right."

I followed his gaze to the sign. The fancy lettering in azure and gold read: *Zazbry's Jewelry Co.* I smiled.

"It's not hard to follow a directory," I said.

"Not what I meant. You're right: it's personal, and I'd appreciate it if we kept things professional."

"No problem, Ace, or is it P.I. East again?"

He rolled his eyes and walked inside the jewelry store. A harmonious chime sounded as we entered. The inside of the shop radiated with the shine of light on metal. Gemstones drew in the eye. It was just like any Zazbry

Hot on the Heels

I'd seen in New York or London, and no less busy on a November weekend.

Ace leaned on a counter and waited. In his suit and tie and me in my trench coat, I realized we might look exactly like a couple in love. An attendant noticed us right away.

"What can I show you today?" a woman in ruby lipstick and a merlot dress asked.

Ace pulled the bag out of his jacket. "We're looking for whoever bought this ring."

The woman, whose gold-plated nametag read: *Lacy, Store Manager*, said, "I'm sorry, all purchases are confidential."

Ace took a card out of the same pocket and handed it to her. "I'm working privately on a case that involved a potential homicide. Anything you can tell me might help bring justice to the victim."

The woman looked between Ace and me. Then, she took the bag and held it up. Her eyes widened a little at the inscription, and she thrust the bag into Ace's hand.

Shaking her head, she said, "I'm sorry, without a receipt, I don't even know if this was purchased in our store. There's another Zazbry's in the city. You might try there."

I shook my head. There was no way I was leaving it at that.

"Can't you look up the inscription or talk to your employees?"

She eyed me with a stern expression. "We're rather busy right now. So, unless you have a warrant or would like to make a purchase—"

"That's all right. We'll just give this over to the authorities. I'm sure they'll want to come back with that warrant. Thank you for your time."

Ace tucked the bag into his pocket again. Placing his hand on the middle of my back, he ushered me out of the store. I stopped right outside and turned. His hand dropped away.

"What was that?" I asked. I put a hand on my forehead. "Never mind, I can guess. You play by the book, and there was nothing else you could do."

"There *was* nothing else I could do."

"You could've pushed a little more."

"I did. I was serious about sharing this with the police. But I've got friends in the department. They'll get a warrant and they'll share their info with me."

"Except that you just tipped her off," I said.

Ace walked farther from the store. "Sometimes the threat of a warrant gets people to open up."

"Not her. She knew something, and she didn't look like she wanted to share it," I said.

We stopped by a kiosk. Ace put a hand to his chin. His eyes wandered over the shopper and back to the store.

"She was startled, which means she didn't know anything about the ring until she saw it just now. But if she recognized something in the inscription, it had to be the name."

"Marc. Maybe she knows him," I said.

"I have a way to get a list of employees," Ace said.

"Hold that thought."

My eyes wandered over the shops and kiosk nearby. I had an idea, the moment I saw a familiar face at a stand just diagonally situation from Zazbry.

I gestured for Ace to follow. Nearing a woman in skinny jeans in a loose, autumn-yellow sweater, I stopped. A few customers were perusing the collections in her kiosk: *Vanity Mirror: Makeup & More.* I waited for her to finish ringing up a customer before stepping into her line of view.

"Victoria? You might not remember me, I'm—"

Her eyes lit up. "Kait! Forget you? Not in a million years." She reached for a hug, which I returned happily. When she parted, her smile remained. "How are you? I haven't seen you in forever."

"I'm all right," I said.

Victoria's eyes traveled to Ace. He nodded, almost as if tipping a hat. I held palm out in his direction.

"This is Aeson East." Then, holding a hand out toward Victoria, I said to Ace, "And this is Victoria Jelant. She's a friend of mine." I was glad that I could call her my friend. Being five years older than me, Victoria had been more like a mentor. When I'd first met her, she had worked in Ava's parents' shoe store while mixing her own cosmetics, which she now sold in her own mall cart. Her vision to one day own a global makeup brand was only a matter of time.

Victoria exuded confidence as she shook Ace's hand. "I taught this world-class model everything she knows about beauty. The trivial things she learned herself," she joked. Victoria had a way of speaking that danced between flippant, charismatic, and serious that captivated people without her really trying.

Ace smiled so that I assumed she'd done the same to him. Then he looked at me with an impatient expression that read: *"And how is this relevant to our case?"* I'd never seen anyone react so little to someone whom I had always thought so amazing. I wondered briefly if he was one of those men who lived and breathed his work. I brought the conversation back to our case.

Hot on the Heels

"Ava is in trouble. A woman fell off the escalator yesterday."

"I heard the screams. What a shame. Wait, how is Ava in trouble? It was an accident, wasn't it?"

"That's what we're trying to find out," Ace said.

"P.I. East is helping me find out what I can about the woman. Do you know who she was?"

"Sure. Penny Hollison, she worked for Ava a little while. Is that why Ava's in trouble?"

It seemed Victoria didn't know about Penny's transgressions. But at least she knew her. That led me to my next question, though Ace beat me to the asking.

"Do you know if she was ever in Zazbry's?"

"Only all the time," Victoria said. "Her fiancé worked there."

Ace and I looked at each other.

Then he turned to her, asking, "Was his name Marc by any chance?"

She nodded. "Marc Winterby."

"I'm guessing he's not here today. He's probably at home grieving," I said.

"You'd be guessing right, but there's a whole lot more to the story."

"What do you know?" I asked Victoria.

She took a few steps away from the cash register. There were still one or two people browsing her shop, so she kept her voice down.

"Two months ago, Penny visited Zazbry with another man—while Marc was working there. I'm not sure what the gentleman bought her, but you don't make eyes like that if you're not in love—if not with the man, then at least with the jewelry."

"Any idea who he was?" I asked.

"I've seen him around, but I don't know his name."

"When was this?" Ace asked.

"Two months ago. But here's the stranger part: Penny and Marc broke up only two days ago. They were still together a whole month while Marc knew Penny was cheating, and he only seemed to care about it recently."

"Maybe they broke up and got back together before that." I shrugged.

Victoria shook her head. "Penny was a customer. I mixed a special foundation for her, and I can tell you this: Makeup is personal. You don't trust just anyone with it. Penny trusted me, and I could tell she wasn't in love with that man who was with her. She loved Marc—even when she was cheating on him."

Hot on the Heels

"Thanks for your help, Victoria. We'll have to get together sometime soon." I exchanged a hug with her and turned to leave.

Ace tapped my elbow.

"Wait. I'll check Winterby's home. You stay here and see if you can get any updates from your friend, Ava."

I had a feeling he was trying to protect me, which some might consider chivalrous, but I found it irksome. I would have argued, but I had my own reasons for staying anyway. I wanted to check in with Ava. If ever a person needed a friend, she needed me now.

Chapter 6

Deal Breaker

I meant to see Ava. Could I help it if I needed some coffee first? And the best coffee shops just happened to be on the fourth floor, near GlamShoe Maven. Once I was up there, I figured it didn't hurt to go in.

The difference between Sensational Soles and GlamShoe Maven was the posh presentation. Whereas Sensational Soles had a selection of high-end shoes, everything here looked like it was one of a kind, with the price tag to match. Only it wasn't. I knew designer, and these were not it.

The black walls made the shoes stand out, as did the bit of sparkle on the otherwise black floor. Some faux jewelry attracted customers to tables in between displays of sale items in the back.

Hot on the Heels

I noticed a few shoes that were awfully similar to the ones at Sensational Soles. One set of pumps in particular caught my eye. Marked higher than most other items in the shop, and fancier, too, the pair of pumps had a quality to them that I had seen the day before: a pink diamond heel.

Ava had said that the pumps were part of an exclusive deal. I picked it up. Close examination revealed how similar it was to the original design. Based on the untarnished heel, I concluded it was a close copy.

"You have excellent taste," a voice said from behind me. A raven-haired gentleman with gray at the temples in a midnight-blue suit greeted me with a smile. "That's one of our own designs, a GlamShoe Maven original."

"Is it? Because it's similar to a pair I saw in Sensational Soles," I said.

His brown eyes narrowed. He lifted a shoe and pointed to the logo branded into the soles, saying, "Spark Heels is GlamShoe's brand. I assure you, unlike what you might find in our competitors' shops, our shoes are unique designs created from a talented woman, my sister, Marge Maven."

I slipped the shoe back onto the slot in the wall. "I heard about her passing. I'm very sorry to hear that she's gone."

He swallowed. His eyes teared enough for me to conclude that he may have cared for his sister. Or was that guilt tugging at the corners of his mouth? He stopped himself before his emotions got the better of him.

Clearing his throat, he said, "She will be missed, but we all must carry on to keep this store moving forward, as she would have wanted."

"I'm sorry, I didn't get your name."

"Drew Maven." He extended a hand.

I shook it with a sympathetic look. "I'm sorry for your loss."

"Yes, it was unfortunate."

"I heard she was in her forties—a bit young for a heart attack. Did she have a heart condition?"

"She must've had one, but we weren't aware of it. If you'll excuse me, this topic is a little sensitive." He turned to walk away.

"Of course. It's just...I really can't understand why I saw these shoes at Sensational Soles."

"Because they're thieves and we have a right to sue them if they continue."

The gruffness of his voice swayed from the image of a gentleman he presented. I was getting to him. So, I continued.

Hot on the Heels

"The thing is, I heard you had an employee committing espionage against Maven's company. That employee died earlier this morning."

The man's eyebrows raised. "Who are you?"

I stepped closer, extending my hand. "Kaitlynn Sasse, I'm working with a private investigator looking into the death of Penny Hollison."

He moved his arms behind his back. "I don't have anything to say about that."

"You can talk to me, or you can talk to the police. I know that Penny was a spy for your sister. The police might be very interested to see the similarity between this shoe and the Ava Price's designs."

"Are you accusing me of something?"

"I have reason to believe Penny Hollison was stealing designs from Sensational Soles for GlamShoe Maven."

He laughed. "You have that backward. Penny was stealing *our* designs for *her*."

He said "Penny" with bitterness. Something about the mention of her name angered him much more than seemed reasonable. While there might be many reasons for an employer to feel strongly about an employee, good or bad, Drew had supposedly only managed the store in the last week. So, why would he have a visceral reaction to Penny Hollison?

He took out a pair of keys with a pink faux-diamond studded S on the chain, saying, "I can prove it" as he walked to the door of GlamShoe Maven's office. He tried the key in the door. It didn't work. He looked the chain over, and his eyes widened. Stuffing the chain into his pocket, he mumbled, "My sister's house keys. I had that mixed up, here it is." He took out his own key set and tried the door again. It opened this time.

Inside his disheveled office, he searched through design books until he found the object of his search. Flipping through a gray sketchbook, he found the design with the pink diamond heel. He tapped the page.

"See? She sketched this one a month before she passed." He closed the book with a snap. I had barely had a chance to glance at it. It looked the same as the one on the shelf, but I couldn't be sure. "Any more questions?" he asked.

"Just one: Didn't you say Penny stole your designs to give to Ava? Why are all of her design books still here?"

His eyes betrayed nothing, but he took at least thirty seconds to respond. Looking as if he had just resuming breathing, he sat against the desk as nonchalantly as an uptight businessman like him could.

"I threatened to sue if Penny didn't return them to me. She did. Then I fired her."

"When did she return them?"

"Not right before she was murdered, if that's what you're implying. I fired her long before that."

"You fired her for spying? Then why state the official reason as petty theft when you know that wasn't true?"

His jaw set, and he looked away. He shook his head in denial, but there were droplets of sweat on his forehead.

"Penny is—*was*—a thief. I saw no reason to get into a legal fight with my competitor. That is, I won't unless they continue stealing my designs. In any case, if you're working with the police, then you know Penny had an addiction. She couldn't help herself. She was even stealing the day she…the day she passed away."

His eyes watered. It was a strange reaction toward an ex-employee-turned-spy. Why would he mourn her passing?

I'd come here suspecting he was a murderer. Now, I was second-guessing my whole view of the situation. He turned, motioning toward the entrance.

"We're done. Please leave my store. Now."

Chapter 7

A New Brand

"He said what?" Ava spared a moment between holiday shoppers to meet with me in her office.

"He accused you of using Penny to spy on GlamShoe Maven. Ava, I have to ask: Is there any truth to his claims?"

Her jaw dropped. She went to the futon, picked up the shoe catalogs, and began rearranging them. After a few seconds, she paused. Then she threw them back down on the cushions and turned.

Pushing the hair out of her face, she said, "How can you even ask that?"

I moved closer.

"I didn't want to. It's just that I know how competitive you can get."

Hot on the Heels

I noticed the portfolio beneath the magazines. My eyes flicked between them and Ava, but her downcast gaze missed it. She put a palm to her forehead.

I felt guilty seeing her like that. I couldn't help but walk over to her and place my hands on her shoulders.

"Oh, Ava, I'm sorry. I should've known you couldn't steal anything. I shouldn't have even asked."

Ava's hand dropped. She gave a half-hearted smile that I knew meant she was still not telling me everything. I pulled her into a side-hug and squeezed.

"Listen," I said as I let go, "why don't we go get some coffee and visit with Scarlett a while? I've wanted to see her bookstore since the changes, and you look like you could use a break. I promise we won't even talk about the investigation."

Ava looked at me blankly for a second, then nodded. "OK, I just have to prep for the afternoon shift change and we can go."

"No problem, I'll be here." I sat in one of the chairs and took out my phone to show I was settling in for the long wait.

She hesitated a moment and then walked out the door, leaving me alone in the office. I waited for the handle to click before standing and walking over to the futon. I went straight for the bottom of the pile, where some loose pages were stuffed between magazines. Flipping pages, I was impressed with the designs. Architectural wheels, pumps mixing new materials, most of it showed promise if not ingenuity. The logo on the front cover was the Sensational Sole's shoe with wings, and there was nothing to suggest the designs originated from anywhere but Ava's mind. I sifted through the catalogs. Standard shoe brands, they suggested nothing out of the ordinary, either. That is until I came across one addressed to GlamShoe Maven.

Ava had Marge's mail, and that suggested she might have other items belonging to Marge, too: like her designs. With all these catalogs sitting out in the open, the police might jump to the same conclusions. So, why were they out in the open? It dawned on me that Ava might have been searching for something. A catalog? A design? Or was there something inside one of these that might be incriminating?

I flipped through the booklets, looking to find something written inside or a sticky note. Suddenly, I saw a tip of white from the corner of my eye. I bent to look under the futon and found a business card. I picked it up and dusted it off.

Hot Heels Shoe Manufacturers, it read. An appointment date and time was scribbled onto it in blue pen. It was the date and time Ava and I had headed back to the store before being bumped off by Penny's demise. She'd said she'd had a meeting, the question was, was it a meeting to create her own shoe line or to steal Marge's? Luckily, I knew a private detective who might help me find out.

I thrust the magazines back into a pile as I heard the door handle snap open behind me. Taking two steps forward to the window, I acted as if I'd gotten up to have a look at the falling snow. I noticed a picture of all of us girlfriends together at a housewarming party for Ava when she'd first purchased her home in the Catskill Mountains. The warm memories it brought to heart and mind told me my old friend couldn't be guilty. I shifted my gaze back to the front door when I heard Ava come in.

"Ready to go?" she asked.

"Yeah," I said, walking to the chair to grab my coat and ruby-red purse.

She moved around her desk, taking her bag from the drawer and extracting a set of keys. As she slid the drawer back, she must have seen the confusion scrawled across my face.

"I had a new set made. Let's go the back way."

We traveled through a back corridor located on the other side of an "Employee Only" exit door. The exit sat inside Sensational Soles only a few paces away from Ava's office. The hallways were narrow and had a lower quality tiling. Still, they were wide enough for the two of us and even had tables and chairs, restrooms, an elevator, and vending machines. We went upstairs, landing on the fourth floor in front of a set of double doors. They opened out to the main hall between GlamShoe Maven and the public restrooms.

"Convenient," I said.

"Too close for comfort, you mean. Ella Belle could have suggested we move to a location much farther from each other rather than going straight to threatening us with eviction."

"The proximity must've made it easier for Penny to spy on you, maybe even to swipe your keys."

Ava gave a pained expression. We walked toward the end of the mall, far from GlamShoe Maven without Ava speaking. I waited for the discomfort to force any words out of her.

"About Penny," Ava said, when we finally reached Sycamore Books.

I faced her. She breathed deep.

"Penny was spying, but not for Marge."

"For you?" I asked.

Hot on the Heels

Ava crossed the threshold. Sycamore Books was exactly as I remembered it: the rows of old knotty pine bookshelves, the kid's area with the mushroom chairs and tree stump branches and stage area for the story time readings, and, my personal favorite, the café in the back.

We met Scarlett at the entrance to the café and she took a few minutes to make three lattés, then she sat with us. Only then did Ava continue her revelation.

"Penny wasn't spying for me. It was for herself or maybe someone else. I don't know whom."

"How do you know it wasn't Marge?" I asked.

"Because Marge and I already knew each other's designs, knew each other's records, all of it."

Was Ava admitting to mutual spying or was there something else going on? Scarlett, always wiser than me, saw it more clearly.

"So you were going into business together?" Scarlett asked as she took a sip of her latté.

"We decided competing would just put us both out of business. Despite public perception, GlamShoe Maven was dying, too. The only reason they seem to be expanding is because my store was going to merge with hers and I'd own half of GlamShoe Maven."

"Why hers and not yours?" I asked.

Scarlett answered that one. "Marge Maven built her store into a staple of the Blue Diamond Mall. Her name is recognizable even outside Diamond Springs."

"Which only makes my case harder," Ava said. "There's already been some speculation about Marge's death. I was with Marge just an hour before she died. I usually used the back corridor, but I'd just fired Penny, and I was upset enough to storm in through the storefront. Penny had just told me that Marge had been contracting with companies behind my back. She was trying to cut me out of the deal. I should have known Penny was lying, that she was trying to turn us against each other."

"Why?"

"I don't know. Maybe to turn the blame away from her. For all I know, she killed Marge Maven."

"Ava, Marge's heart attack was no one's fault."

"I know. But what timing!" Ava pushed her coffee away with a look as if she was sick to her stomach. I knew she wasn't just thinking about business. Even as a competitor, Marge seemed to have earned the respect and friendship of her co-workers. The heart attack had come as a shock, but knowing the events surrounding it, the timing did seem odd. I just wasn't sure the reason why.

Hot on the Heels

"Terrible timing because of the launch of your shoe line?" I asked.

"Apparently, Drew beat me to that," Ava sighed.

"I don't understand, if you own half of GlamShoe Maven, then why are you still competing?" I asked.

"Marge and I hadn't signed anything yet. We had a contract but kept adjusting it. We were still working out details."

"Then, when she died, you had no proof of a soon-to-be merger?" Scarlett asked.

"Plenty. Emails, text messages, and even a contractor we'd both seen together—Hot Heels Manufacturing. But Drew said none of it was legally binding. He's not obligated to honor any of Marge's promises, and he's technically right about that."

"But the designs are yours?" I asked.

"Yes and no. Marge and I worked together to create Spark Heels. All the designs were ones we came up with in brainstorming sessions. She'd draw in her notebook and I in mine, and we'd compare sketches."

"Your notebook would be proof of your collaboration then, wouldn't it?" Scarlett asked.

Ava turned redder by the second. "Yes. The pink heels—I have the rough sketch of them in my book. Marge and I both had versions of the final. We went with mine. I could absolutely prove it—if I could find the book."

Realization struck. "That's why you have your catalogs and those loose portfolio pages out all over your office?"

"Right. The pages were designs I was working on recently, but my design notebook isn't there."

"How long has it been gone?" Scarlett asked.

"I haven't been able to find it since Penny's death."

Ava, Scarlett, and I all shared a look of horror. We sat silently, sipping our coffees and staring at the ground. I tried to think about the possibilities.

"What color was your sketchbook?" I asked.

"Red. Why?"

"Drew Maven has a gray one in his office."

She nodded. "Marge's was gray."

"So, Drew doesn't have your notebook, then," Scarlett said.

"I'm not ruling it out just yet," I said. I turned to Ava. "Do you have any proof the design was yours besides the book?"

Ava shrugged. "The Hot Heels Manufacturer. Marge paid the deposit, but I was the one who worked with the representative on the design. I also paid the second shipment, but I was never charged for it and it never came in. I had a call scheduled with him—that's why I cut our lunch short. But then, Penny, well, you know.... Anyway, the manufacturer rep is on his honeymoon with his secretary, a.k.a. wife #3, so I haven't been able to get a hold of him to prove anything."

Ava's eyes began to well. Those tears may have been in part for Penny, Ava was not compassionless, but they were also a culmination of her frustration. She might lose the business her parents had built from scratch and the legacy she had hoped to make her own.

Scarlett put a hand on Ava's. I wrapped an arm around her shoulder to offer my support.

"That representative will get back eventually. Then you'll have the proof you need. People like Drew might think they can get away with lies, but the truth always comes out in the end."

Ava sat up straight, as if finding new resolve. "Drew Maven is a ruthless businessman. He wants GlamShoe Maven to dominate Blue Diamond Mall and he doesn't care who he hurts in the process. But he can't hurt me. Spark Heels is mine."

Chapter 8

Leave a Penny

I met Ace in a bar on West Main Street. It was not my ideal location. I never liked bars. They had less of the sophistication of breweries and fancy restaurants. This one on Main Street was a rustic, log cabin-type design for which I didn't care.

I changed at home before coming. A tan pantsuit with red heels might attract less attention than a dress if we were going undercover. But also, the weather had been taking a turn throughout the day. By now, with the sun falling, it was chilly.

I set my purse down on the counter and waved my hand as the bartender looked at me, telling him that I was fine without a drink for now. Ace had a drink in front of him, to which I grimaced. If I'd known Ace East was a drinker, I might not have hired him.

Hot on the Heels

"Don't you think it's a bit early to be drinking?" I asked.

He looked at me disinterestedly. "We're in a bar, it looks less suspicious for me to have something. I asked the bartender to fill it only a quarter of the way, so it looks like I've been at it. You should have one, too."

"Why?"

"Because Marc Winterby is a regular. He didn't show up to work today. I figure he'll show up here soon."

Ace called a waiter over. I ordered a hot toddy mocktail. If I was going to pretend to drink, I wasn't going to do it with alcohol in the middle of the day. Besides, I hadn't eaten anything since breakfast.

"What about his home?" I asked.

"His roommates said I'd be more likely to find him here."

"Did you think they might be protecting him?"

"From an old friend in town for the weekend?"

Ace smirked. He'd lied, which I'm not sure counted as an ethical violation for an investigator.

"OK, so we're waiting for him to show up?"

"Not just waiting. My informant at the mall just called me back with a tidbit of information that you might find troubling."

Fear tingled at my throat. "What's that?"

"Your friend Ava's business was in the red. Seems she couldn't make it in the new environment. The mall was less than a year away from shutting her down."

I sank in my chair. This only confirmed my suspicions that Ava had been backed into a corner. It was no wonder if she had resorted to stealing.

Ace continued, "Before you get too upset, GlamShoe Maven was facing similar numbers. It looks like they were going to nix one, and the Mavens' business was performing a little better. I'm sorry—but I think the police have a motive if Ava found out about Penny stealing her designs."

"It sounds like you agree with them," I said.

I was changing my mind about telling him that Ava might have been stealing, too. It would only make her look guiltier in his eyes. He took a small sip of his drink.

"He's here," Ace glanced at the door and turned back to face the bar.

I caught a glimpse of a man in a brown shirt, olive bomber jacket, and dark jeans. He ran a hand over his well-trimmed mustache and goatee and let the door shut behind him. Piercing blue eyes almost caught mine in the mirror as he spied the empty seat next to me. I turned my head toward Ace as Marc walked over.

Hot on the Heels

If Ace hadn't said anything a minute ago, I wouldn't have guessed that he'd even noticed Marc Winterby's arrival. He just kept eating peanuts.

Marc raised a hand for the bartender's attention and placed his drink order.

I turned and smiled at him. In situations like this, no matter how distracted or otherwise engaged, I'd found that men generally responded with a light conversation. All I got out of Marc was a tight-lipped smile before his attention went right back to his drink.

"Hi, I'm Kaitlynn," I said with a hint of flirtation.

He glanced at me again with a flat expression. "Look, I'm sure you're as astonishing a person as you look, but I'm just here to drink and catch a few hours away from everything and everyone."

"Sounds like something's on your mind you would rather forget," Ace said, still not looking in Marc's direction.

Marc eyed him a moment. "Yeah, you could say that."

He took a drink. Ace finally turned his eyes toward Marc, then glanced at me. It seemed he wanted me to say something.

I scrambled for words. "I, uh, find it's easier to deal with problems when I talk them out. Care to share?"

He scoffed. "Women. It amazes me how you can talk about everything under the sun but can't say a word when it comes to the truth."

"What do you mean?" I asked.

Ace laughed. "He means his girl was cheating. Am I right?"

Marc scowled. He hesitated to say anything further. Ace turned in a friendly manner, leaning one elbow on the bar as he looked at Marc.

"How long was she going behind your back?"

"Four months."

Ace winced. "Ouch. That's tough. Sorry."

Relaxing into the conversation, Marc said, "The thing is, I saw it this whole time, I just didn't want to see it, you know? Then she said she wanted me back and I..." He paused, took another swig of his drink, and let the words hang.

"So, you knew who it was? Was it a friend or a roommate or something?" I asked.

Ace glared at me, only for a second, so that Marc wouldn't catch it. The roommate comment might have been too on the nose. If Marc caught on to the fact that we knew who he was and that he had roommates, our whole plan to gather information would be compromised. I saw that almost as soon as I said it.

Hot on the Heels

As it turned out, he didn't seem to notice. "It was a rich businessman—only she found out he was poor and came right back to me. So like a woman," he said.

"Not all women are like that," I argued.

Ace's critical look returned. I didn't care. I had to defend my gender, even if this was all just an act.

"If it were me, I might've strung her along a little while, confront her with the truth after pulling her heartstrings a little."

I grimaced. If I didn't know that Ace and I had found the ring, I would think Ace meant what he said. I hoped he was only trying to get more information out of Marc.

"I did, sort of. She knew that I knew about it, but the thing is I wanted to forgive her. I just couldn't."

"So, how'd you make her pay? You did make her pay for it, didn't you?" Ace asked.

Marc pushed his drink aside and stared at Ace. His eyes narrowed as mine widened. If Marc had made Penny pay with her life, he certainly wasn't going to confess it to a stranger in a bar. He'd likely defend himself first— with his fists, possibly.

I scoffed. "Is it my turn to say 'how like a man'? Do you really believe in hurting people back instead of just moving on?"

Marc grabbed his drink again. The tightness in his expression faded.

Ace went back to his drink, too. He muttered before taking the last sip, "If she deserved it."

Marc whispered into his glass, "Maybe she did." He finished off his beer and ordered another.

"Did she?" Ace asked.

This time Marc laughed. It was a bitter laugh that sounded like defeat. His tone was defensive.

"You're with the police, aren't you? I'll tell you what I told the other officers: I didn't have anything to do with Penny's death. I loved her."

Ace pulled his card out of his pocket and slid it across the bar, saying, "I do occasionally work with the police, but I'm not an officer."

"Then I don't have to talk to you."

"But you should," I said. "If you're innocent, we can prove it. It would give you an advantage."

Marc stared at his drink, seeming to consider it. That was a good sign, as I saw it. I kept going.

"It sounds like you were angry with Ms. Hollison. You were seen arguing with her two days prior and broke off your engagement. That might be considered a motive."

Hot on the Heels

"No, if you watch the tape, you'll see I wasn't anywhere near her when she fell. Maybe she was depressed about our engagement ending. She might've killed herself."

"Funny you should mention the mall tapes. They show you having coffee with Ms. Hollison minutes before she died. Care to explain that?" Ace said.

I tried not to show my surprise. Ace had either kept that from me this morning or had spoken with the police in the hours since we'd split up.

"She wanted to meet with me."

"You tried to grab her ring."

"I paid for the ring. It's mine. And I didn't get it back, did I?"

"Marc, we know Penny was poisoned."

Marc's jaw dropped. I tried hard to suppress my growing anger. Couldn't Ace have shared one piece of crucial information with me before confronting a suspect?

Marc shook his head. Despite his olive complexion paling, his voice was firm, "If you look at the recording, you'll see that I never went near her tea."

"Yet you know it's tea?" I asked.

"She always drinks tea. Anyone who knew her knows that."

"Nice try, but you're an employee of the mall. You'd know the locations of the cameras and when they rotate."

"They don't tell us that stuff! We don't even have access to all the back corridors. Are you trying to help me or not?" He sounded incredulous.

I touched his wrist. "If you're innocent, you have nothing to worry about. He's just trying to establish that."

He took a deep breath, closed his eyes, then looked at Ace again. "Look, I didn't drug her. Yes, we had an argument a few days ago, and yes, we met at the café, but only because she wanted to get back together. Part of me wanted to—I still loved her. But I said no."

"Because her cheating hurt you?"

"Of course it did. Have you ever been in love? How would you feel if your girl was cheating on you?"

"Angry. But what I don't understand is why get angry then? Why not two months ago?" Ace said.

"What?" Marc asked.

"Didn't you know about the affair two months ago?"

Marc clammed up. He knew what Victoria had told us. Without saying a word, he'd confirmed it with the beads of sweat that had started forming on his forehead.

Hot on the Heels

He stood and threw a few bills on the table. "Some help. Anything else you want to ask, do it through my lawyer."

He walked out of the bar.

"We made him nervous. He knows he talked too much." Ace stood and paid for the drinks—his and mine, even though I'd barely touched it.

"He didn't exactly confess," I said.

"No, but he gave us plenty of reason to suspect him."

"Do you really think he killed her for cheating on him? Seems kind of cliché."

Ace laughed. "It's cliché because it happens all the time. Love makes people crazy."

My stomach growled as we walked out of the bar. "So does missing lunch. Care to join me for dinner?"

"If you don't mind having it at the office. I've got some paperwork to go through. Maybe you can help."

Chapter 9

Follow the Money

My helping meant hours of pouring over public records with a carton of Chinese food. Ace and I divided up the names of our people of interest, then scoured online databases for more information. I read so many unrelated facts, I could sum up Marc's, Penny's, and Drew's lives.

"Listen to this: Penny Hollison and Marc Winterby have both been arrested before for theft. Guess where they met? A group therapy program for shoplifting addiction. She went on a court order a year ago. So did Marc. And he works in a jewelry store! He had to have lied to get hired there."

"Not necessarily," Ace said absently.

His eyes were glued to his laptop. I pulled another record up on the screen.

Hot on the Heels

"There's also a record of sale for a couple of properties Drew Maven had in New York City."

"That's not unusual; people sell investment properties all the time."

"All of them? The county recorders only have him on record for one property: a home in Diamond Springs he bought two months ago."

"Those records aren't always up-to-date. We need something major, like bankruptcy. Use the list of databases I gave you to look that up."

"Sure, give me a minute."

I shifted through the paperwork on the non-existent secretary's desk. I grimaced at what must have been a week-old, empty take-out container and threw it away. A little organizing allowed me to concentrate. Finally, I searched and found a list for public bankruptcy and financial records databases online.

"Looks like your suspicions were right. Drew declared bankruptcy this year," I said.

"Interesting," Ace murmured.

I let go of the mouse and waited. Ace put a hand on his chin and leaned back in his chair. His *"man of few words"* quality was starting to annoy me.

"Care to share what's 'interesting'?"

"I have a contact at the mall who gave me a very helpful tip just before I left to look for Marc," he said.

My lips thinned. He'd failed to mention the tidbit about having a mall informant when we'd visited the mall earlier, and it would have been nice to know he was interviewing this person before we split up. In fairness, he'd only met me less than twenty-four hours ago, and I assumed P.I.'s didn't reveal their sources to anyone.

"What's the tip?" I asked.

"Marge Maven's store was sinking almost as much Ava's."

"Ava told me that. But everyone else seemed to think GlamShoe Maven was thriving."

"It wasn't, according to my source. Her store was going to close next year if she didn't make some drastic changes. She'd planned to take on a silent partner to stay afloat," Ace said.

"Yes, I heard. Did your source tell you who it was?" I hoped that there might be someone out there who could confirm Ava's pending merger with Marge.

"Marge had a meeting scheduled with my informant last week, but she died the day before. My source tells me she suspected it might be the brother, since he arrived in town around the time Marge was talking about launching a shoe line."

Hot on the Heels

So, the informant was a "she." It was a woman who was privy to the financial standings of stores at the Blue Diamond Mall. I mentally filed that away as important.

"That seems convenient," I said. "Especially for someone who might want to inherit the store without a partner."

"You're thinking Drew. Did anyone contest the transfer of Marge's store to him?"

"No, but if they were just in the negotiating stage, this silent partner wouldn't have any legal grounds to contest the inheritance." Ace tapped his finger on the desk, his eyes crinkling like he was forming an idea. He pointed at my computer. "Wait a minute, when exactly did Drew Maven declare bankruptcy?"

I clicked on the paperwork and scrolled. My eyes skimmed the date. *May 1*, it read.

"Uh, about six months ago."

He snapped his fingers and laughed. "Talk about coincidence."

"Care to share?"

He leaned forward, tapping the desk with a pen for emphasis as he explained, "Marge Maven died on October 13. Do you know how long it takes for inheritance not to pass to a bankruptcy estate?"

I smiled. No, I didn't know, but I could guess: six months. I didn't know much about detective work, either, but I'd read enough Agatha Christie novels and watched enough mystery shows to learn at least one thing: that was a motive.

"I'll call my police contact with our suspicions. Maybe they've come to the same conclusion."

Chapter 10

A Hard Sell

The police had not come to the same conclusion as Ace and I had. By the time we learned they had arrested Ava and hurried over, she was already sitting in an interrogation room. Her eyes were redder and skin paler than I'd ever seen her. In this small town, things were informal enough that Officer Hart allowed Ace and me to question Ava and see some of the evidence against her.

Jones was deep into his interrogation. His files, sitting closed on the table, I assumed held some evidence of her guilt. Or at least, whatever they had might look like it pointed to her. Hart, Ace, and I piled into the room as Ava pleaded her case.

"I told you. Yes, I did go to meet with Marge the day she died, but her brother was there, not her. He said she'd had a heart attack earlier that day. I didn't see her before that."

"And you didn't steal her designs?"

"Everyone knew that in the last year, Marge was taking on a silent partner. What no one knew is that it was Ava," I explained.

Ava nodded. "Marge and I have been working on it for a year. The first shoes were supposed to be ready for sale in December."

"And in all that time, no contract?"

"We were drafting one."

"For a year? That's a stretch."

"A merger is no small undertaking," I offered.

Ava said, "I trusted Marge."

"Until Penny tried to turn you against each other by stealing those designs and claiming she was cutting you out of the deal. And you believed her."

"No!" She put her head in her hands. Then she continued, "Yes, but only briefly. The moment I found out she'd had a heart attack, I regretted ever thinking she could do something like that. We were friends. But don't you see? Penny was giving those designs to someone else. I don't know who."

"What I see, Miss Price, is that you killed Marge Maven to keep the brand for yourself and killed Penny to keep her from taking those designs to her partner in crime."

"No! Marge had a heart attack, and I fired Penny. And that was the end of it. Marge being dead doesn't help me at all. Her brother told me right in my office that my store was trash and that he wouldn't taint GlamShoe Maven with any brand that came from my 'second rate mind.'"

"But you and Maven were negotiating a contract with a shoe manufacturer together?" Jones asked.

"Yes, until her death."

"And you say this manufacturer has proof you were the designer?"

"Not proof, just conversations. I did most of the design work, and we told him that," Ava said.

Officer Hart interrupted, "You're right, Miss Price. He confirmed that much to us on the phone. Even honeymooners pick up the phone for the police. But I'm sorry, it only proved my suspicion. He said that despite GlamShoe Maven paying for the shoes, he had directions to send the prototype shoe to you. You instructed him specifically to send all shipments your store, not Marge's, so I think I can reasonably conclude you were trying to cut her out of the deal."

"I can explain that. Marge's brother was visiting, so she didn't have time to deal with approving the prototypes. She wanted me to take charge. Besides, once Marge died, Drew called and changed the delivery address so that the shipments went to GlamShoe Maven. He moved up the delivery date. Marge and I weren't planning to release the shoe until January. We had to correct an issue with the prototype: The heels snapped under the slightest pressure. Yet Drew is selling those same shoes three months early. Wouldn't you call that suspicious? I'm telling you Marge's death doesn't benefit me. If she were still alive, I'd have 50 percent of her company!"

"Her failing company. You're right that you don't have a chance of getting her company now that she has passed, but you do have a chance at taking the Spark Heels brand now that she's dead," Hart said.

"Maven's store brand was still worth more than Ava's. Her shoe line would have had a better chance as a product of GlamShoe Maven than Sensational Soles, which means Ava was getting the better end of the deal. I don't think you have your culprit," Ace said.

"Then, who is it?" Hart looked us in the eyes as if daring us to accuse someone.

"What about the boyfriend?" Ace said. "Did you investigate him?"

"We went to his home. He had stolen merchandise from both GlamShoe and Sensational Soles. He says they were Penny's."

"He has a shoplifting record, too. He was likely involved in Penny's conspiracy to steal the shoe designs," Ace said.

"Or she was working with Drew. Marc said she'd left him for a rich man, who she just recently found out wasn't as rich as he claimed. That's a near-perfect description of Drew Maven."

Hart smiled. "Yes, you were kind enough to suggest yesterday that we investigate Mr. Maven on suspicion of poisoning his sister. We found something curious."

Jones opened a file and pointed to a picture. I recognized it as the one of us together at Ava's cabin home. Jones pointed to a shrub in the front yard.

"Oleander: also known as a poison said to mimic heart attacks. The flavor is masked in tea, which Marge liked to drink daily. It was found in her system when we tested her body. And it grows abundantly on your property," Jones said.

Ava shook her head. "I replanted a year ago, all those shrubs in the front yard are gone. Check the cabin if you don't believe me."

"We did," Hard said, "and we found plenty of it in the backyard."

While the officers were concentrating on the shrubs in the picture, my eyes caught something else— something that could prove Ava's innocence. I picked up the picture and stared. Everyone in the room noticed the light bulb switching on in my mind. It all started to click.

"I think I know who it is. Do you have tapes on all the areas Miss Hollison visited the day she died?"

"Just of the fall. We could only trace her steps back to the jewelry store. She disappears before that," Jones said.

"I think I know why. Do you have any cameras of the back corridors behind the stores?"

"Not the interior themselves, but the mall would have all entrances and exits to those areas," Hart said.

"Good. With your permission, I'd like to check the tapes with you as soon as the mall opens tomorrow."

"Tomorrow is Black Friday, Miss Sasse. I hope you have a good reason to bother mall security. What exactly is it you think you'll find?"

"The key to solving this case."

Chapter 11

Black Friday

After reviewing the tapes, we headed straight for GlamShoe Maven. Drew, dressed once again in a clean-cut stylish black suit, stood answering customers' questions when we cornered him to ask him ours. Hart and Jones in full uniform, Ace in yet another wrinkly suit, and me in a green pantsuit ensemble, we waited patiently for him to finish his dialogue. When he was done, he couldn't help but notice us.

"Miss Sasse, officers, to what do I owe the pleasure?"

"We'd like to see that shipment of Spark Heels you had in the back," Officer Hart said.

"It is the busiest shopping day of the year. Could we not do this another time?" he asked. Hart stared him down. He turned, saying, "Of course, right this way."

Drew led us to the back room past dozens of shoppers. As we neared the door, he took out his keys. They slid easily into the handle and turned the lock. I pointed to the keychain.

"What happened to Marge's keys? The ones with the pink swirled S? I think you said they were her home keys?"

Drew regarded the keys in his hand and stuffed them into his pocket. He opened the door, moving into natural conversation.

"Right. I took those to her home, naturally."

"We're going to need those, too," Officer Hart said.

"Of course." Drew smiled.

It was the deceptive smile of a man I knew was going to pretend to "misplace" those keys later. But from what little I'd observed of Drew, he'd hold on to anything he thought had a chance of still being useful. Plus, he wasn't exactly a criminal mastermind. He had enough hubris to believe he could get away with murder. A man like that wasn't careful enough to cover up his crimes.

Jones looked through the books and boxes of shoes. I began to worry it was a long shot. Then I remembered he'd put the keys into the desk.

"Top drawer," I whispered.

Hot on the Heels

"Would you mind opening the drawer?" Hart asked Drew.

Drew huffed as we walked to the back. "You do know it's Black Friday, don't you? It's the busiest shopping day of the year."

"I don't think you'll care about that so much in a second," Ace said.

Drew opened the drawer. It was empty. So, I'd underestimated him. Or, possibly, I hadn't.

Ace snapped his fingers. He asked to see Drew's keychain. He reluctantly handed them over, not without complaint. Ace took them with the tip of a pen he'd taken off the desk.

"I can't see what this is going to solve."

He handed the set to Ace.

Ace held it up to me. "You saw this keychain yesterday. How many keys would you say were on it then?"

I smirked. "There are three extra ones now."

"I'll bet those fit in Ava Price's old office lock, her safe, and her home," Officer Hart said.

Hart snapped a rubber glove onto his right hand and took the keyset. Jones came up behind drew with a pair of handcuffs. Drew swirled around.

His eyes widened, and he sputtered, "What exactly do you think you're doing?"

"Arresting you," Jones said.

Hart began, "Mr. Maven, you have the right to remain silent—"

Drew jerked his hands away. "I will not. I think I have the right to know why I'm under arrest."

"I think you know exactly why," I said.

Drew scoffed. Then, looking at the officers, he said, "Is this your source of information? Of course, she'd accuse me of something. She wants to help her friend."

"I did help my friend, by discovering exactly how you killed your sister and Penny Hollison."

He laughed, addressing the two officers and ignoring me. "This is preposterous. You can't believe I would kill *my own sister?*"

Ace said, "You would if it meant inheriting this store. You saw this as your way out of the debt of your own failed businesses."

"This one is failing too!" He moved around the desk, closer to Ace and the officers. "I admit Marge and I have covered it fairly well, but I'm sure you could have uncovered that with a little research."

Hot on the Heels

"We uncovered a lot with surprisingly little research. For instance, mall surveillance reveals that you did see Penny Hollison minutes before she died," Hart explained.

"I certainly did not!" He jerked his hands away from Jones' attempt to cuff him again. "Absolutely no camera in this mall would show that."

I stepped forward. "You went into the employee access door just outside your store. Penny went into the one from inside Ava's store. She came out a minute later at the food court."

"So? How is any of that related to her death—or to each other for that matter?"

"Her cup of tea," I said.

His reaction showed it all. He took out the pocket handkerchief and dabbed his forehead. He said nothing.

Ace chimed in, "There's a tea and coffee machine in the back corridors stretching from here to there. It's located right by GlamShoe Maven. You had to have seen her."

He paused. Placing the handkerchief back in his pocket, he straightened.

"Oh, yes. I recall it now. It was hardly worth mentioning. I went for a morning coffee, and I saw Penny at the machine."

"Where you assaulted her? Perhaps you broke her shoe, causing her to later trip and fall to her death," Officer Hart said.

"Not at all. I saw it as a chance to tell her that there were no hard feelings. I even bought her the tea."

Ace said, "I'm glad you admit that. But again, you made an error of omission."

"What omission? I've told you everything now."

"Except the most vital part," I said. "You poisoned Penny Hollison's tea."

He looked as if he might curl his fingers and throw a punch, but it was just a flicker. Soon, it turned into a laugh. "That's rich. What would possibly lead you to conclude that?"

"The fact that you did the same to your sister," I said. I felt intimidated by the way he leaned forward just enough so that it looked like he might spring an attack on me any second. But I couldn't back down.

He shook his head. "Again, on what evidence are you basing this?"

"White oleander," Hart answered.

Jones added, "It was in both your sister's and Hollison's bodies."

"You should've had your sister cremated," Ace said.

Hot on the Heels

Drew shook his head. "That only proves that the same person, Ava, killed both of them. She had a motive."

"But not opportunity. You were there in both cases. And you had access to oleander from the keys we just found on your keyset. They're the same ones Penny stole for you so that you could get into Ava's office and her home. You hatched the plan when you went to Ava's office. The oleander bush was in plain view in a picture on the wall."

Hart moved in closer to an increasingly agitated Drew.

"We looked into your many failed business ventures. One of which was with a natural medicine company, an apothecary shop of some sort. You had some experience with herbs and medicines. You could have recognized the oleander and saw your opportunity."

Ace chimed in, "Marge wanted to keep you out of the company affairs, even asking Ava to handle the prototype and shipment of their joint brand to keep it away from you. Perhaps it was because of your poor ability as a businessman, or perhaps it was because she feared you. Either way, you killed Marge to take over her thriving company, only to realize too late her business was going under, just like yours had."

"Pure speculation," he said.

"At first it was pure speculation that led me to it. It was something Penny's fiancé said. He said that Penny was with a rich man until she found out he was poor. That's a perfect description of you," I said.

"That's a lie. She was never with me for my money. She—" he paused, realizing he'd let something slip.

"That's reasonable suspicion. Arrest him, Jones," Hart ordered.

Drew pushed Hart into Jones. Then, he flung the office door open and made a run for it. Knocking over a display, he dashed out of the store and through the mall. Jones and Hart pursued him. Grabbing an employee as he went, Drew threw her into the officers and continued into the crowd.

Ace moved ahead of me and gave Hart a hand.

"You OK?" he asked.

"It had to be a mall on a Black Friday?" Hart asked. "We'll never catch him in the crowd."

Chapter 12

On a Spree

"**I** see him. He's going downstairs," Jones said, resuming the chase.

Hart sprinted behind.

I wasn't going to run in high heels. Ace helped the woman who had fallen. When she was standing, he put a hand to his chin. Strategizing—I liked it better than making a blind dash for it.

"What are you thinking?" I asked.

"He has to make it to an exit," Ace said.

"Third floor has the employee parking lot," said the woman that Drew had tripped.

Ace began walking. "Will you call and get security on the exits?" he asked as he and I left the store.

The woman nodded and hurried to the phones behind the registers.

"There's an elevator in the exterior corridor," I said.

"I'll go, you stay here," Ace said.

Men seemed to think they were being gallant when they gave orders like that. I wasn't having it. I walked in step with him, letting my heels do the arguing as they pounded against the floor. He glanced sideways at me, but at least he knew better than to say anything.

We made it to the elevator in seconds. Ace pushed the button before a janitor could make it inside. I raised one angry eyebrow at him.

"It's dangerous, and we're in a hurry," he explained.

"No excuse for poor manners, besides, I have an idea of where he's going," I muttered.

It was true. I knew from being in these corridors with Ava that it led to the upper-level employee parking. We would have plenty of time to spare. I wondered why Drew hadn't thought of using this himself. Then again, waiting for an elevator wasn't exactly a way to outrun a chase.

That wasn't it, though. It wasn't panic leading him. I knew my thinking was right once the doors opened on the ground floor. Gasps and frightened shoppers stopping in their tracks made it easy to spot Drew and his hostage coming.

Hot on the Heels

All he had was a pocket knife, but jabbing into Marc's neck, it was enough of a threat to keep Jones and Hart from closing in on them.

I caught sight of Hart by the fountain with his hands hovering near the hilt of his gun. "Think carefully, Drew. You don't want to do this. There are hundreds of witnesses and nowhere to go from here."

"Oh, yes there is. You're going to let me walk to my car and drive away or he's going to pay for what he did right here and now."

The look in Drew's eyes turned to wild rage when mall security swarmed around them, blocking the exits. Ace and I left the elevator to make a slow and steady approach.

Everyone else around him froze.

"He's going to kill him," I whispered.

Ace continued moving forward, though I was doubting if that was still a good idea. Drew jabbed the knife deep enough into Marc's neck to break skin. Marc's eyes filled with fear and he stopped struggling against his attacker's grip.

Drew shouted, "Stay back!"

Ace kept going. I tried to make my own steps as unnoticeable as possible. Drew hadn't looked this way yet, and there were enough shoppers between us that he might not have seen us.

"He's getting close to your friend," Ace observed.

Seconds after Ace's comment, I saw Drew and Marc walking close to Victoria's cart, The Vanity Mirror. He was heading to the mall exit.

That meant that he was also coming toward us. He was sure to spot us soon, but his eyes were on Victoria. I couldn't see her face, but imagined she had a combination of fear and anger coloring her features. She always had a fiery nature, which might be why Drew widened the distance between them.

With Drew preoccupied by Victoria, Ace took his chance. He darted around the kiosk. I held my breath as I hoped against hope that he could surprise Drew by circling behind.

The movement was enough to cause Drew to turn. He saw Ace coming. Drew pushed Marc toward Ace, thinking he'd found a weaker hostage in a woman running a makeup cart. I knew better.

"Victoria, look out!" I screamed.

Knowing my friend, I prayed she'd put her years of self-defense classes to use.

She did.

Hot on the Heels

Her foot stuck out and caught Drew's ankle. As Drew instinctively thrust his hands out to brace for the fall, she grabbed his arm and flipped him Krav Maga style. He landed face-first against the marble floor.

Officer Hart took advantage of Drew's fall to yank his hands behind his back and cuff him. Officer Jones took Marc's arm, too. He tugged away.

"Hey! I'm the victim, what are you doing?"

"You're under arrest for theft and conspiracy to commit theft of intellectual property," Jones said.

"You have no proof of that," Marc spat.

"Not much, no. All we have is a tape showing Penny holding four bags before going having coffee with you, and three when she left. You walked away with the fourth," Officer Hart said.

"Yeah, she gave me a bag. How was I supposed to know the stuff in there was stolen?"

I said, "You'd have to know it that Ava Price's sketchbook wasn't something Penny purchased. We can see the red leather binder sticking out of the bag in the video."

"Funny, we didn't find any red leather binder in your house. I suspect we'll find it in your employee locker," Officer Jones said.

Jones moved to complete the arrest. Marc leaned away, as if he might try to run like Drew had. Victoria moved into Marc's path. He hesitated, no doubt contemplating the danger posed by Victoria's heels and how she could use them. That faux pas gave Ace the chance he needed to spring behind him and pull his hands behind his back and right into Officer Jones' open handcuffs. Two clicks later, the case was closed.

Chapter 13
Bang for the Buck

As Officer Hart led Drew out, the disgraced storeowner struggled.

"You're making a mistake!" he said.

"You ran," Ace replied.

"Because I was being framed." Drew looked at me. "She planted those keys on me!"

I smirked at the obvious floundering attempt to pin the blame on me. I was surprised to see Hart and Jones' faces clouding with doubt about the accusation. At least Ace wasn't fooled.

"Save it. You ran because you were guilty."

"Slanderer!" he shouted.

My heart beat faster. I needed the officers to have as much faith in me as Ace had. But what could I say that would prove my innocence?

Drew kept shouting, "You'll regret this. I'll sue you all. You don't know who you're arresting!"

That was it! I took my chance—"Just like Penny didn't know who she was rejecting?"

His eyes reddened with rage.

"She thought you were poor, a sham, and, frankly, not worth her time. She didn't know what you had planned. She didn't know everything you were doing and had done for GlamShoe Maven," I pushed.

He spoke with fire, "She said she loved me. Then she changed her mind. How could she do that to me? To me! I would have built an empire. I'd have given her everything. But she chose to go sniveling back to him! She had to pay."

Drew jolted as if he were going to leap at Marc again. Hart pulled him back. He and Jones had heard enough.

"All right, keep moving," Hart ordered.

"You can tell us all about it at the station," Jones added.

I laughed. The breath escaped my lungs like a rush for freedom. I reached out to Victoria for a hug, sharing the joy and relief radiating through me.

"You were marvelous!" I said.

"Thank you. You weren't so bad yourself." Victoria eyed Ace as he walked up to a security guard who was urging the crowd with pleas of "there's nothing to see here." I spied the guard handing Ace a walky-talky. He was probably communicating with his mysterious female informant. I still wondered who that could be.

Victoria nudged my shoulder, saying, "You seemed to make a good team with that dashing detective." She smirked. I nudged her right back.

"Private detective. And I plead the fifth on whether or not I find him dashing."

Ella Belle seemed to come out of nowhere from the crowd. An entourage of more security guards followed her. She pointed to the officers and the security guards circled them, escorting them out of the mall. No doubt they'd stick with them through the parking lot in case the culprits tried to flee again. Ella walked right up to Ace, speaking with him for a minute.

"Does Ella know him?" Victoria asked.

I didn't answer except to say I'd see her later. Instead, I walked up to Ace. Ella turned. She pursed her lips and nodded. That was as close to a "good job" as I was ever going to get from her. Then, she walked away.

"So, Ella is your informant?" I asked.

"Yes." He grinned. "She told me the two had a less than friendly relationship."

"And what kind of relationship is yours?"

"A working one," he said.

"Meaning that it's strictly work, or that you have something special and it works for both of you?" I teased.

"You seem unnaturally interested in my love life." He gave me that narrow-eyed detective look, like he was homing in on the truth.

"I'm naturally inquisitive."

I put a hand on my hip, enjoying how his smirk spread into a smile. He turned, putting his hands in his pockets as if nothing at all had happened to us today. We began walking toward the mall exit.

He said, "Still, we should keep a certain amount of professional distance."

"Does that mean I get the job?" I asked.

"What job?" He played innocent, but I knew his game.

"The one I'm pretty sure you've been testing me for since we met."

He winked. "You're sharp enough; I'll give you that."

"You'll give me at least what I made before and health benefits if you want me to stick with you."

He grinned. "Congratulations, Miss Sasse. You're my new secretary."

"Associate," I said.

"Assistant," he countered.

"Executive Assistant." I crossed my arms.

"What's the difference?"

"It's closer to the real job title I'm accepting today."

"Oh? What's that?"

"Future partner."

He chuckled. "You start Monday, 8:00 a.m. sharp. Don't be late."

"I'm always on time and dressed to a T. You can count on that, Ace."

Chapter 14

Setting up Shop

Doorbells are reminders that we live among friends. Mine rang several times as all the members of my girl squad arrived at my "glad to be home" bash. Forget the parties in New York and London, this topped them all.

I was especially glad when Victoria appeared at the door. I owed her one.

"Victoria, thanks for coming."

"I wouldn't miss it." She handed me a small package wrapped in blue paper and a pink ribbon.

"What's this?" I asked.

"A welcome home gift. Open it," she said.

I pulled the string and tugged at the paper. Lifting the lid revealed a row of business cards. I pulled one out.

Hot on the Heels

"Kaitlynn Sasse, Executive Assistant to Ace East, Private Investigator. These are wonderful. Thank you!" The gold trim and engraved letters complemented the smooth texture of the cards. It had an officiality to it that made my move here finally sink in. I really was home.

"It's nothing. Just a small thank you for saving my life."

"How'd you get them done so fast? I just told you about the job yesterday."

"Had them do a same day delivery so I could pick them up while I was picking up my own."

She pulled a card out of her jacket. I took it. Rose gold and thick, the card had a swish of glitter swirling across the vertical word: *VICTRESS*. On the opposite side was gold lettering, with her title as CEO and founder.

My mouth opened wide as my lips raised. "Your own makeup line?"

She beamed. "It launches this May, at the grand opening of a new department store: Coraline's."

"Coraline's? That's a major chain—congrats!"

"Well, they're only trying it out at this location for now. But once it shows promise here, it'll go regional and then national."

"It's going to be amazing."

I hugged her and left to set the cards down in the sitting room. I placed it on end table beside the sofa. I should have had a better spot, tucked away from sight, but I tended to forget about things if I didn't see them.

Case in point was the envelope I'd sat there with my mail earlier: the one from Titania Talent Agency. I picked it up. With no one in the room at the moment, I had a chance to open it. I ripped the envelope and read the letter.

"Something interesting?" Ava joined me.

"Yes." I turned around. "It's a job for a resort fashion week in New York in May."

"Are you going to take it?"

I looked behind Ava at all the women gathered in the living room. A part of me did miss the thrill of the catwalk, but it was no comparison to my friends in the Catskills. Especially on nights like tonight, where the snow was falling and the fireplace crackled in the background while we all shared stories about what was going on in our lives.

Maybe when May came around, I could take a week's vacation. A fashion show here or there might be fun. As for a full-time job, Executive Assistant to Ace East, Private Investigator, sounded more exciting than the runway.

Hot on the Heels

I stuffed the paper back in the envelope and said, "I already have a job, and there's a certain P.I. in Diamond Springs who needs my help more than he knows."

Want more great content?

Hi, I'm Astoria Wright, the author of A Sassy Sleuth's Mystery series. I hope you've enjoyed Book 1: Hot on the Heels.

Check out the rest of
A Sassy Sleuth's Mystery series:
Hot on the Heels
Head Over Heels
Heels Dug In

Check out Astoria Wright's other series,
The Faerie Apothecary Mysteries:
Chaos in the Countryside
Herbs and Homicide
Remedy and Ruins
Elixirs and Elves
Charms and Changelings
Potions and Panic
Talismans and Turmoil
Tonics and Turning Points

To keep up-to-date about this series and others by the author, check out the website:

www.astoriawright.com

Sign up for the mailing list for updates and freebies available only to members!

Thanks for reading!